This book belongs to

LINNIE VON SKY

Pom Pom
A FLIGHTLESS
BULLY TALE

✳

illustrations by R. A. BENDER

Silk Web Publishing

Did you know that Antarctica is our planet's southernmost continent? Here's some trivia* you may want to store forever.

Fact: there are no ants in Antarctica.

*triv·i·a: tiny specs of seemingly useless information used by children to impress adults

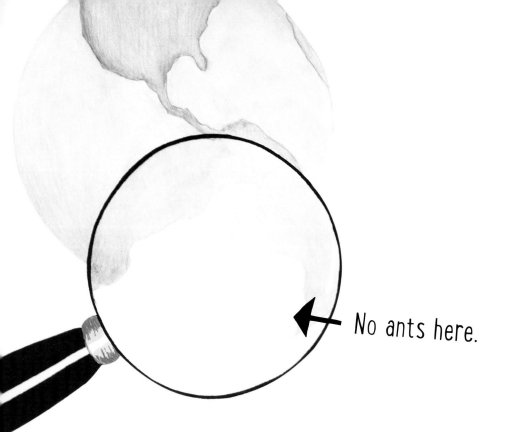

No ants here.

At least the **smart people** with big magnifying glasses who search for our earth's species have not spotted an Antarctic ant, and that's a good thing, because I **don't** particularly like ants and I live, you guessed it, in Antarctica.

And this •
over here
is me!

I like you, so I'll tell you a secret. Ants scare me a bit. They make my feathers **fluff with fear** when they crawl around in my thoughts.

Will you please not tell the others? My dad says only **imbeciles** are afraid of ants. I am not sure what that means, but in my imagination I guess it's a grown up word for "stupid", because that's how he makes me feel when he calls me that.

Ever since I was a little macaroni penguin
(yeah, yeah... I am still a little penguin, though
no longer a little chick penguin), my family
and friends have called me **Pom Pom**
for short.

Since we're only just meeting I'll tell you another secret. I don't really love it when they call me Pom Pom. I'd rather they use my real name: Pomeroy Paulus Junior III.

Hahahahaha

The others think it's **funny.**
They quack at me all the
time: "**Hahaha** you are as
round as a Pom Pom. It's
really quite perfect that
your name is Pom Pom".
You would think that
joke would get old. Well it
doesn't. Not to them.
Not ever.

In fact, they seem to think it's the funniest thing since burnt toast, and they often laugh so hard that they have to hold their bellies until they get a bad case of hiccups and end up sliding around on their backs with their wings flapping and their feet waving.

Hahahahahaha

Hahaha

Mom calls it **mocking.** I'm not sure what that means, but in my imagination I guess it's a grown up word for "not really funny" because I don't think it is.

Sometimes I **laugh along** because it's really no fun to be the only one not laughing. But really, I'll tell you, I truly don't get **why it's funny.**

Mom says friendship is when you laugh together, but if truth be told my friends only ever really seem to laugh **at me.** Come to think of it, so do dad, my cousin Percy, Nanna Peach, and my sister Polly.

Maybe mocking is a grown up word for "they don't really love you". At least that's how I feel when they call me Pom Pom and hoot like owls holding their belly feathers so they don't shake off.

The other day at swim class I saw the world's most amazing surf trunks. The orange ones Pucker wears... they are so cool; Piper, Peter, and the other penguin boys have the same pair and I have wanted them

Pia!

← Pucker

for months! I will tell you another secret, since I know you won't tell. Pia said they were her favourite when she saw Pucker wear them and now I kind of hope she'll say the same thing to me.

Mom is really awesome. She bought a pair of new orange surf trunks, took a piece of orange rubber, sewed it in, and now **they fit me.** You can hardly notice the difference. You see, they never really carry my size at the big **Ant-A-Mart** in town. It's a good thing mom's so crafty.

❁ My awesome mommy ❁

Peter

Today when we met for swimming lessons by the glacier pond I felt a little **prouder than proud.** I pushed my chest out a little, because that's what Pucker does and I've heard him say that the "birds love that". I can't imagine that the seagulls really do love that, but maybe it will work with Pia and it can't hurt to try.

The next part of my story makes me remember the fair last summer when my ocean blue helium balloon floated off into the clouds right after dad had bought it for me. The knot magically untied itself from my wing tip and off it went into the sky. My good mood popped with a loud bang, and it hurt like someone poked me with a needle on the inside.

Mom says the first part of what happened this morning is **cringey.** I'm not sure what that means, but in my imagination it's grown up talk for what happened with my balloon, but many times infinity **worse.**

When I arrived at swim class I had an extra little skip in my step. I was wearing my new orange surf trunks and when I ran past the others to cannonball into the ice cold waves in front of Pia, it happened.

Maybe I had my chest out a little too far because my feet slipped a bit, my flippers waved a lot, and I lost my balance. Silly me, I knocked myself onto my feather bum, split my new orange surf trunks right down the middle (in the back...luckily), and plopped into the ocean like a sack of wet herring*. That instant I wished I could have dived under the floe of ice and swum all the way over to Australia where the ants live.

*he-rr-ing: little fish with really shiny bodies that are puffins' favourite delicacy

Rrrrip Crack

Galapagos*

Australia

I heard my class
burst their tuxedos
at the seams with
laughter all the
way into the depths
of the ocean.

*Ga-la-pa-gos: where the frigatebirds live

But, worst of all, I heard Pia's lovely voice giggle behind her elegant penguin wing. Nothing could have saved me. I, Pomeroy Paulus Junior III, remain afraid of ants and thus Australia was out of the question. I had to face the laughter.

♡ Pia ♡

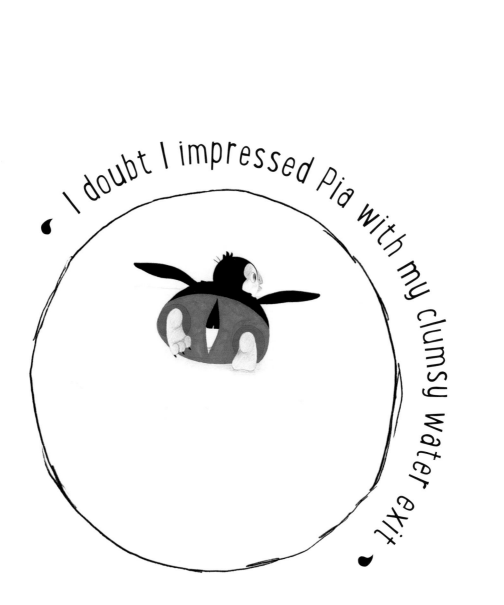

I doubt I impressed Pia with my clumsy water exit.

When I jumped back onto the ice carpet I heard Pucker and Piper. "Pom Pom is a macaroni penguin because he is made of mac 'n' cheese" Pucker snorted.

Then Piper turned to Pia and gargled "maybe Pom Pom should have saved the last twenty **beaks full** of breakfast for later because then his **big plump bum** would not have burst out of his giant orange **tent trunks** for all of us to see".

Just when I felt like the **red hot shame** would rise into my head and the **tear water** that lived there would have to come out of my eyes, Pia **redefined magic.** She reached for her towel while **she danced** past Piper (oh what a fine-looking macaroni penguin she is) and strode toward me. She put her towel **around** my hips and her wing around my shoulders and stared Piper, Pucker, and the rest of the class straight in the face.

She raised her lovely voice and said
"Real friends don't ever laugh at friends.
Mocking (there it was again that big word

and it sounded **so good** coming from her) is for **weaklings** and I like my friends **strong, gentle and brave**".

With that we waddled away with her arm around my macaroni penguin shoulders. I can truly say that I have never pushed my chest out so **proud.** To me Pia was the **strongest, gentlest,** and **bravest** penguin of them all.

That evening when mom **kissed** me good night she said I am **lucky** because in Pia, I have finally found a **true friend.**

The Happy End*

It's time to lend my voice to my many incredible friends and family members who have felt tiny because of the way others (strangers, and sadly, friends and family) have treated them over the years. Let's love and respect unconditionally with zero tolerance for weight bullies. — Linnie

— Rebecca

Pom Pom A Flightless Bully Tale — Pomeroy Paulus Jr III wants two things in life: his friends and family to stop calling him 'Pom Pom' and to impress Pia with his new orange surf trunks. A children's tale about kindness, friendship, empathy, love, and respect.

First published in hardback in Canada by Silk Web Publishing in 2014.

Text and illustration copyright © 2014 by Linnie von Sky.
Illustrated by R. A. Bender — Rebecca hand-illustrated Pom Pom A Flightless Bully Tale in watercolour and pencil crayon.

Type is set in *Cassia* and *LunchBox*.

Printed and bound by Friesens in Altona, Canada on FSC ® certified paper using vegetable-based ink.

Cataloguing data available from Library and Archives Canada.

isbn 978-0-9919612-1-4 (bound)

Author: Linnie von Sky; Illustrator: R.A. Bender; Editor: Taisha Garby; Book Designer: Christina Leist.
Digitalization of Rebecca's original drawings magically done by Imagine This Photographics Inc.
Thank you my lovely Stephanie Cox for your help with digital file preparations.

This is a testament to the awesomeness of those who made our second *publishing dream fly:*
Mom and Dad, Angela Alberga, Dunsi Oladele, Maddi and Jenn Co-McMillen, Kevin Mwangi, Linda Mofford, Redfish Kids, Scott Wilson, Sean Wharton, Shandra Taylor, and Michael and Sandi Lyon.

Introducing the custom characters and an extra sprinkle of gratitude:
Harriot the Owl for Christine Sharma
Snowman the Snow Leopard for Arya M. Sharma
Lillebror the Polar Bear for Rashmi Sharma
Simon the Seewuwu for Kamala Sharma
Magnus the Mammoth for Paul and Lori
Wow-wa the Husky for Julie + Ron Hall's beloved granddaughter Arianna
Dewey the Fox for Brian Stonehocker's beloved nieces Emily, Ali, Chloe, and Rachel + his nephew Chase Leavitt
Hank the Eagle for the Obesity Action Coalition
Juji the Jack Russel for Frank Taleghani's beloved daughter Sadie
Kalle the touque wearing Hummingbird for Sylvie + Frank Scherzer's beloved family Lilith, Samuel Elias, Jette, Neo + Jan

Pomeroy and Pia are dedicated to Karen Suffern's darling twins Ryan and Amber. Thank you for being so incredibly brave. I sure wish the world had more courageous people like you two in it. - Linnie

MIX
Paper from responsible sources
FSC® C016245
www.fsc.org

Visit us at www.linnievonsky.com